The Food Pyramid Disaster

Bonnie Broccoli

Mark Milk

Sammy Salmon

Wanda Wheat Bread

Sweetie Soda

Candy Bar

Charlie Chip

Jason

Judy

Officer Garcia

A busy street

Bonnie Broccoli: Boo hoo! No one likes me.

Mark Milk: What is the matter, Bonnie Broccoli? Why are you crying?

Bonnie: Kids will not eat me. They say I taste yucky!

Sammy Salmon: The same thing happens to me. They make faces when I am served for dinner. They say, "You taste fishy." Well, I should. I am a fish!

Mark: I know what you mean. It is a fight to get kids to drink me. I have to let them mix in chocolate syrup.

Wanda Wheat Bread: Kids think I taste bad just because I am healthier to eat than white bread. But I taste good!

Sweetie Soda: That is a laugh. Kids don't want to eat whole-grain breads, veggies, and fish.

Candy Bar: They want to eat sweets, like me!

Charlie Chip: And fatty foods like me!

Sweetie: Then wash them down with sweet drinks, like me. You healthy foods are a bunch of losers!

Bonnie: That's it! I'm tired of everyone making fun of me.

Mark: Me too!

Sammy: Me, three!

Candy: What are you going to do about it?

Sammy: Leave the food pyramid!

Bonnie: Good idea, Sammy Salmon. Let's go where we are wanted.

Wanda: I'm with you. Let's get out of here!

Charlie: Go ahead!

Sweetie: Yeah, who needs you?

Candy: Now kids will eat even more chips, candy, and soda.

Charlie: It will be a party at every meal!

Bonnie: That's what you think. You're going to be in trouble without us.

Sweetie: We'll be just fine.

Bonnie: I don't think so. Without us healthy foods around, the food pyramid will be out of balance. You will fall over.

Wanda: Just watch. Here I go.

Candy: Hey! What are you doing?

Bonnie: We're leaving! Good-bye, Candy, Charlie, and Sweetie.

Mark and **Sammy:** Bye, junk foods!

Candy: Whoa! Now that those foods left the pyramid, we're tipping over. Help! Help! Ouch!

Charlie: Ow! That hurt. And I just crushed my favorite snack. BBQ-flavored chips!

Candy: And look! I spilled jelly beans all over the road.

Sweetie: And I spilled soda all the way across the street.

Wanda: What a mess! People are slipping on the greasy foods.

Mark: And now they are getting stuck to the sticky foods.

Bonnie: No cars can get through.

Sammy: The whole town is stopped! Crowds are forming.

Jason: Judy, look! What is going on here?

Judy: I'll look in a second, after I take another lick of my ice cream cone. Yum.

Jason: That does look good. I should have gotten sprinkles on my ice cream cone.

Judy: But you already have hot fudge and marshmallows.

Candy: Hi, kids. I'm glad you are enjoying your sweet treat. But as you can see, there is food all over the road.

Sweetie: We need your help.

Jason: I just have a little bit left. Mmm. Now, what do you need us to do?

Sweetie: The healthy foods left the food pyramid. The rest of us foods lost our balance and fell down. Can you help us get back up and fix the food pyramid?

Jason: Let's give it a try, Judy. One, two, three, lift. These pieces are heavy!

Judy: Grunt! Groan!

Jason: We're not strong enough.

Candy: Try again, please. For me?

Judy: It's too hard! I'm out of breath!

Jason: I need to rest. Maybe if I had a piece of candy, I'd have more energy.

Bonnie: If you kids ate healthy foods and exercised more, you would be stronger.

Jason: Healthy foods? Like what?

Sammy: Fish and lean meats.

Bonnie: Fruits and vegetables.

Jason: I was afraid you were going to say that.

Wanda: Try whole-grain breads and cereals for breakfast. That's a very important meal, you know.

Judy: I don't want to eat all that healthy stuff. It doesn't taste good.

Bonnie, Mark, Sammy, and **Wanda:** Here we go again!

Officer Garcia: Okay, everyone. Settle down. I'm Officer Garcia. What happened here?

Candy: The healthy foods got tired of people saying they taste bad. So they left the food pyramid.

Charlie: The rest of us foods lost our balance. We fell over!

Officer Garcia: I'll help you up. Uh . . . whew . . . you guys are heavy. I . . . puff . . . can't do it.

Sammy: You must be eating too much junk food too, Officer.

Officer Garcia: Well, I do eat cookies and donuts sometimes.

Wanda: Sometimes?

Officer Garcia: Okay, I eat them a lot.

Sammy: Adults don't eat enough healthy foods, either. We sure have our work cut out for us.

Bonnie: You kids say you don't like healthy foods. But have you ever tried them?

Jason and **Judy:** No.

Bonnie: Why not?

Jason and **Judy:** We never see them advertised on TV!

Mark: You know, if you kids ate healthy foods, you'd feel better. Your bones and muscles would grow stronger.

Sammy: You would have more energy. You could play longer without getting tired.

Jason: I like the sound of that!

Sammy: And you would do better in school.

Judy: I like that idea, too.

Officer Garcia: And if I was in better shape, I wouldn't get out of breath chasing down bad guys. Maybe it is time to try some healthy foods.

Jason: I will if you will. Here goes.

Bonnie: Try some of me.

Judy: Gee, this broccoli is kind of crunchy. And it tastes good!

Jason: Yeah! The fish is delicious! And I didn't have to make a yucky face.

Officer Garcia: I love the chewy crust of this whole-grain bread.

Jason, Judy, and **Office Garcia:** More healthy foods, please!

Bonnie, Mark, Sammy, and **Wanda:** We told you we were good!

Sweetie: I was wrong about you healthy foods. I am sorry I teased you.

Charlie and **Candy:** Us, too. But now we are stuck!

Jason: For awhile. I have an idea. Judy and I will start to eat healthy foods.

Judy: Yes! We will exercise more, too. Soon we will get strong enough to lift up the food pyramid. Will you healthy foods come back then?

Bonnie, Sammy, Mark, and **Wanda:** We thought you would never ask.

Officer Garcia: I will rope off this area for the next few weeks. I will put up a sign: "On vacation."

Jason and **Judy:** From junk food!

Candy: Boo hoo! Now I am going to cry.

Bonnie: Don't worry, Candy. It's okay to eat sweets once in awhile.

Mark: Just not all the time. That's why you are the smallest part of the food pyramid.

Wanda: Breads, veggies, and fruits are the biggest and most important part.

Sammy: Then comes milk, meat, and beans.

Candy: And I am last. Treats are the least important part of the food pyramid.

Jason: We still like you, Candy. We won't forget you.

Judy: Or Charlie and Sweetie.

Jason: And when we come back, we'll lift you up.

Judy: The food pyramid will be back together.

Office Garcia: The foods will be balanced again.

Judy and **Jason:** And you treats will taste even better than ever.

The End